Toby was left staring at himself in the mirror. His eyes took
in his messy hair and mismatched pyjamas and Toby noticed
that he was smiling. He might not look like his friends, but he
looked like a lot of fun! He closed his eyes and remembered
the feeling of flying and the dazzling colours of the ocean. He
glanced back into the mirror and liked what he saw -
the magnificent Toby Plum!

Before he could thank his new friend, the town square faded
away and Toby found himself back in bed. The sun was just
rising through the window. He looked around frantically for
Differ, calling his name and peering out the window.
There was no sign of him. Toby jumped out of bed to check
the hall, but as he passed the mirror he saw Differ staring
back at him. "I thought I would never see you again,"
Toby said, relieved. "Don't worry, my friend," Differ whispered
with a grin. "Whenever you need me, I'll be here in a jiffy."
"Oh Differ, I had the most wonderful adventure!" Toby gushed.
Differ waved and said "I will see you soon, Mr. Plum"
as he faded away.

Laughing so hard tears came to his eyes, Toby sat down next to a pair of old ladies. His eyelids began to feel heavy. Flashes of his adventures swept through his mind. Beautiful snowflakes and wonderful fish. Scary lizards and magical birds. Dull, terrifying Sameville and, most amazingly, all the fantastic people in his own town square.
He felt a hand on his elbow. Turning, he saw Differ wink at him.

Differ peered at Toby. "Look a bit closer, my friend."
Toby squinted his eyes, but he still couldn't see it.
He looked at all the people of different sizes, shapes and
colours. They laughed and joked happily.
He watched mums and dads with cuddly babies.
He gazed at the groups of moody teenagers and
the cute old grannies nattering on the bench.
Toby suddenly understood. PEOPLE. Differ was right.
They were beautiful. All of them were amazing in
their own special way. Their differences made
them magnificent! Toby laughed and laughed.

Toby started to hear the gentle hum and bustle of lots of different sounds. He heard the whoosh of a bus and the beep of a lorry's horn. He looked around and noticed dogs playing, birds tweeting and squirrels scavenging. He then began to notice lots and lots of people, hundreds of them bustling from here to there. Toby soon realised that he was standing in his own town's main square. Babies laughed and cooed and old ladies gossiped on the benches. Mums and Dads played with their kids, throwing them into the air and catching them again. Huddled groups of teenagers mumbled quietly. Toby looked baffled. "Differ, where is this amazing and magnificent animal? I can only see people."

Toby perked up. Another adventure was
just what he needed. "What is it, Differ?"
"Oh you just wait, Mr. Plum. You just wait."
Toby felt a familiar tug as Sameville
thankfully faded away.

Back on the playground, Toby looked up to the sky. He gasped. All the birds looked exactly the same! They sang the same tune and flew at the same height. Baffled, Toby ran over to a small stream at the back of the yard. He peered down, only to see that all the fish were the same, too. No collection of beautiful colours, no groups of various sizes, nothing! Just boring, grey fish swimming in straight lines. As Toby was looking into the water, he suddenly noticed his reflection. He looked identical to all the other boys in the school! He jumped back from the stream, horrified. "Differ!" he yelled.

Differ tapped Toby on the back. "What's wrong, Mr. Plum?" "Differ please get me out of this horrible, boring place. There is no colour, no laughter! I don't want to stay here." Differ looked confused. "But Mr. Plum, I thought this was your wish." Toby remembered how he had felt when he looked in the mirror. It felt like ages ago. "I've changed my mind Differ," he declared. "I want to be back in my body! Please let me go home." Toby began to whimper. "Please don't cry, Mr. Plum. We have one more stop. We are going to see the most beautiful animal in the whole world. It comes in all shapes and sizes and each one is magnificent in its own special way."

Toby strolled over to the school and snuck into one of the classrooms.
The teacher, who looked like a grown up version of all the kids,
was handing out test results. Toby loved getting test results,
as he was quite smart and always worked hard.
He loved learning about science and nature. When Toby looked around,
he saw that each student had received the exact same mark.
None of the students were happy or disappointed.
They just seemed lifeless. Toby ran out of the strange, dull classroom.

"What is this place, Differ?" Toby asked.
"Well, Toby, this place is called 'Sameville'.
There are no differences here. Have a look around and see what you think.
If you like it, you can stay here forever and you will never have to feel
different again." Confused, Toby began to explore.
He wandered over to the racing track and noticed that a race was starting.
All the kids ran at exactly the same speed and crossed the finishing line
at the same time. What was the point of racing if you never ever won,
no matter how hard you tried? Why would you ever even practice
or try to get better?

They landed in what appeared to be a school playground.
Toby looked around. The school building was just like Toby's school.
The playground was just like Toby's playground. It was full of children
playing games just like he played. However, as Toby looked at the children,
he noticed something most peculiar. Each and every child looked exactly
the same! All the boys had black hair like his friend John, they were the
same height as Stephen and wore the same t-shirt, jeans and trainers
as Jimmy. Most surprisingly of all, they had the same faces!
He looked at the girls and saw that they were completely identical too.

As they flew through the air, they encountered birds
of all shapes and sizes, each one just as impressive
as the next. A little robin chirped a beautiful song as
he made his way to the top of a tree. A huge eagle
soared quietly above their heads and then quickly
dove to the ground before flying back up to
the sky. Woodpeckers hammered their beaks
against enormous trunks. Magpies glistened
magnificently black, white and emerald
green. The birds all had different types of
beaks and wings and feathers and feet to do
different things. The big ones were majestic,
but the small ones were exquisite. Each one
was beautifully unique. Just as Toby was
thinking about this, Differ grabbed his
hand and they swooped low to avoid
a flock of hungry seagulls. Toby
laughed as the seagulls screeched
past. He turned to Differ to share
his thoughts, but Differ was
concentrating on the ground
below them. Slowly they
floated back
to earth.

The cloud above Toby's head began to fade. As he held tightly onto the branch, Differ said, "Jump off the tree. I promise you will be able to fly like a bird." Toby gaped at him. Even though he was scared, he knew that Differ had taken care of him so far. He slowly made his way to the edge of the branch, took a deep breath and closed his eyes.

Toby jumped with all his might and started flapping his arms wildly. One moment his stomach felt like a stone, the next he felt light as a feather and began flying higher and higher. "I can fly! I can fly!" he shouted. "I feel free as a bird." Differ quickly caught up and they flew side by side through the sky. It was cooler up there. Soon Toby saw that they were passing over huge forests and enormous rivers. Even in all of his books, Toby had never seen nature like this before!

Toby was still trying to find the little lizard when he noticed a
shadow fall across the sand. Differ screamed. "What's wrong?"
Toby asked, wide-eyed. Differ just trembled and pointed behind Toby.
When Toby looked around, he saw a giant lizard, one hundred
times the size of the little one, making its way towards them.
Toby was excited, as lizards had always fascinated him.
However, he could see that Differ was terrified and so they
both climbed up the tree and rested on a branch.

"Don't worry, Differ. Those lizards won't hurt you.
They are such beautiful creatures! There are so many different kinds.
It's amazing!" Toby could have talked for hours about lizards,
but before he knew it, they were on the move again.

As they looked around Toby could not see life anywhere in the desert, just one lonely big tree in the distance. They quickly made their way over to the tree and plonked down in the shade. As they looked around, something rustled the sand. Toby held tightly onto Differ.
All of a sudden a weird little green head with black beady eyes popped up. Differ was terrified, but Toby grinned. "Oh, Differ don't be scared. It's only a little lizard. I read about them in my nature book and have always wanted to meet one. Hello little lizard!" The Lizard stared curiously at Toby. As fast as he had appeared, he was gone, buried underneath the sand.

Sadly, Differ soon motioned that it was time to go.
Although Toby would have liked to stay in the sea forever,
he was excited to see what lay ahead. Toby waved goodbye
to his new friend the Dolphin and they began swimming
up to the surface.

Toby looked around and saw only sea. "Where are we going
next, Differ?" Toby asked eagerly. "Just you wait, Mr. Plum,"
Differ replied. The water turned a beautiful golden colour
and dissolved into grains of sand. Toby saw he was in the
middle of a vast desert. The sun beamed down on their heads
and Toby began to sweat. Again, Differ whooshed his big tail
and muttered a few strange words. A little cloud formed above
Toby's head and began to rain on him. At first Toby was scared,
but he realised that the rain kept him cool. He smiled at Differ,
relieved to have his very own cloud.

Toby and Differ swam gleefully past huge whales and tiny rainbow fish,
scary sharks and gentle seahorses, playful dolphins and grumpy stingrays.
The mixture of all the creatures' shapes, sizes and colours made the ocean more
beautiful than Toby had ever imagined. "They're all so different and beautiful,"
he thought to himself. Just then, one of the playful dolphins popped up
beneath Toby's feet. "Hop on and grab its fin" Differ shouted.
Toby climbed onto the dolphin and took hold of its big shiny fin.
With that the dolphin shot off through the sea,
swimming at the speed of lightening.
Toby screamed with delight.

Toby closed his eyes and imagined the one place he had always wanted to go. The mountains began to melt away and water rapidly rose from beneath their feet. Toby grew frightened as the water rose higher and higher until finally it was above their heads. Toby gasped, but Differ whooshed his big tail again and suddenly Toby felt gills spring from his neck. He could breathe underwater like a fish! Toby had always wanted to swim deep in the ocean and now his dream had come true. Differ and Toby swam to their hearts' content, passing hundreds of underwater creatures.

"Hmm I can't pick one Differ; they are all beautiful
in their own way". Differ smiled and then rolled all
the snowflakes into a ball and playful threw it at Toby,
"Snowball fight" he shouted with glee and with that
they both broke into a brilliant game of snow fight.

After playing for what seemed like hours, Differ grabbed
Toby's hand again. "Toby, think of anywhere in the whole
wide world you would like to go."

It began to snow. Big thick snowflakes fell lightly onto their heads.
Differ began jumping wildly, gathering snowflakes in his hand.
He ran over to Toby and pulled him close. "Look Toby," he said.
"Each snowflake is a different size and shape. No two snowflakes
in the whole world are the same. Which one do you like best?"
Toby looked closely at the snowflakes and soon realised that
the difference of each one was really magnificent.

Just before they hit the ground, Toby felt a "whoosh"
of air past his head and he suddenly found himself
surrounded by enormous, snow-covered mountains.
The mountaintops soared above Toby's head and made
zigzag shapes against the big blue sky. Toby and Differ
stood side-by-side, frozen in awe. Toby began to shiver
and Differ whooshed his tail, muttering a few words to himself.
Suddenly, Toby's whole body was covered in thick, brown hair.
Toby looked at his furry hand and started to scream,
but then he realised that the hair was keeping him warm.
"Mmm... cosy", said Differ.

At that moment, before
Toby could say a word;
Differ grabbed his hand and
pulled him out the window.

They stood face to face.
"Hello, my name is Toby Plum," said Toby as he extended his hand.
In an odd squeaky voice, the creature answered, "Hello, my name is Differ"
and with that he stuck out his foot and shook Toby's hand with it.
He talked with great excitement.
"Toby, I am here tonight to bring you on an amazing adventure.
We are going to travel to places that you have hardly dreamt of".

Toby closed his eyes and tried to wake up, but when he opened them, the creature was still outside the window. Toby smiled and the little creature smiled back, at least Toby thought the way his mouth twisted must be a kind of smile.
Then, quick as lightning, the creature ran down the branch and jumped into Toby's room!

After a few moments hiding behind the curtains, Toby decided to quietly peek again. As he slowly made his way back to the windowsill, something scurried up the tree outside. When Toby looked a second time, there he was, the little creature sitting on a branch looking straight at him. Was he dreaming?

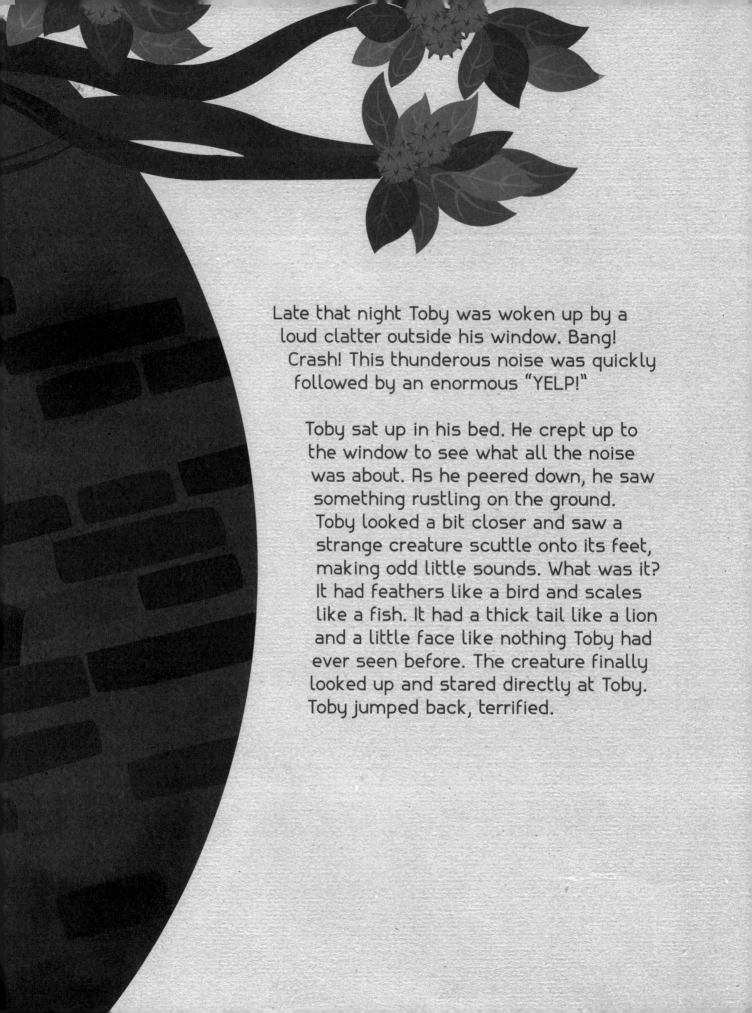

Late that night Toby was woken up by a loud clatter outside his window. Bang! Crash! This thunderous noise was quickly followed by an enormous "YELP!"

Toby sat up in his bed. He crept up to the window to see what all the noise was about. As he peered down, he saw something rustling on the ground. Toby looked a bit closer and saw a strange creature scuttle onto its feet, making odd little sounds. What was it? It had feathers like a bird and scales like a fish. It had a thick tail like a lion and a little face like nothing Toby had ever seen before. The creature finally looked up and stared directly at Toby. Toby jumped back, terrified.

Toby climbed into bed feeling very down in the dumps. He closed his eyes and imagined how happy he would be if he had different hair and clothes. He imagined how good he would feel if he was as tall as his friends. He smiled at the thought of beating Stephen in arm wrestling. But he quickly became sad again when he realised that he could never change that much. He slowly drifted off into a troubled sleep.

Toby Plum sighed loudly as he looked in the mirror. He was not happy with what he saw. His hair wasn't spiky or black like his friend John's. He was far too small. He couldn't jump nearly as high as his friend Paul. He wasn't as strong as his best friend Stephen and his clothes never made him look as cool as Jimmy. Toby wished he could be just like everyone else.

Written by Deirdre Ryan and Deirdre Cowman
info@magnificentlyu.com
Illustrations by Isabel Reyes Feeney
www.isabelreyesfeeney.com
ISBN: 978-0-9568222-0-8

Published by

Magnificently U is dedicated to improving children's self esteem through
encouraging positive body image and an appreciation of diversity. Please
visit www.magnificentlyu.com for more information on children's body
image and lots of Toby Plum activities!

Magnificently U
River Lodge, Rock Road, Bilberry, Waterford
Email: info@magnificentlyu.com
Web: www.magnificentlyu.com

A Donation from the proceeds of the sale of this book will be made to

Bodywhys is the national voluntary organization supporting people affected
by eating disorders. Bodywhys is committed to the belief that people with
eating disorders can and do recover. To find out more visit www.bodywhys.ie

The Magnificent Toby Plum

By Deirdre Ryan and Deirdre Cowman

Illustrations by Isabel Reyes Feeney

This Book Belongs to